CHRISTMAS IN THE MILITARY

Sue Carabine

Illustrations by
Shauna Mooney Kawasaki

GIBBS SMITH
TO ENRICH AND INSPIRE HUMANKIND

Salt Lake City | Charleston | Santa Fe | Santa Barbara

13 12 11 10   6 5 4 3
Text and illustrations © 2003 Gibbs Smith, Publisher

Published by
Gibbs Smith
P.O. Box 667
Layton, Utah 84041

1.800.835.4993 orders
www.gibbs-smith.com

Designed and produced by TTA Design
Printed and bound in China
Gibbs Smith books are printed on either recycled, 100% post-consumer waste, FSC-certified papers or on paper produced from a 100% certified sustainable forest/controlled wood source.

ISBN 13: 978-1-58685-274-0
ISBN 10: 1-58685-274-4

'Twas the night before Christmas,
and Nick couldn't believe
All the letters and cards
he'd just lately received.

Looking closely, he saw
the majority came
From children whose writings
seemed almost the same.

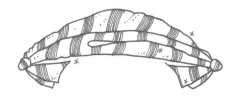

The gifts that they wanted
were not for themselves—
Would Nick find their folks,
with some help from his elves?

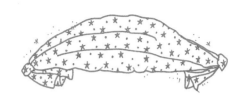

"Our parents are part of
U.S. military forces.
Just help them be happy,"
cried thousands of voices.

"Protecting their country,
they feel very proud,
But we miss them so much
that we're under a cloud!"

Well, Santa's kind heart
was quite touched by their words.
"If I fail to do something,
'twould be quite absurd."

He began making plans
(something special this year),
Kissed his dear wife goodbye,
and then left with his deer.

As they flew through the skies
on this sparkling night,
Nick re-read a letter
of a little boy's plight.

"Dear Santa," it started,
"My first name is Tim,
My dad flies a jet,
but I'm lonely for him.

"Mom sent his gifts early
with Sue's and Bob's too,
But mine would be special
if he got it from you."

He'd made a small compass
from twigs and green clay,
His note said, "For you, Dad,
so you won't lose your way."

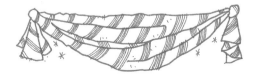

Nick laughed to himself, quipped,
"Now, this should be fun!
Are we ready to fly, boys?
Let's visit Top Gun!"

They sped on their way,
quite a sight to be seen,
And soon cruised beside
a swift-winged F-16.

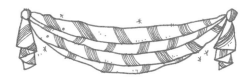

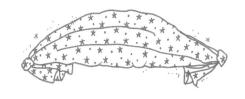

Tim's dad (code name: "Blaster")
could not quite believe
The sight from his cockpit
on this Christmas Eve:

He saw Santa waving,
a grin on his face,
Looking almost as though
he was itching to race.

Nick held up a package
for "Blaster" to see,
Who magically found
the gift there on his knee!

He unwrapped the package,
then read Timmy's card,
And a warm feeling started
way deep in his heart.

He'd been feeling sorry
and quite sad, it is true:
No family at Christmas
makes anyone blue.

You wouldn't find Christmas
bells, stockings, or fun
In a cockpit like this one
while flying Mach 1!

He saluted St. Nick,
and said, "While I'm away,
Make sure that my family
enjoys Christmas Day!"

"Now that was a challenge,"
Nick called to his deer,
"But it's not going to get
any easier, I fear.

"The next request asks us
to dive way down deep,
This young man serves proudly
our U.S. Navy fleet!

"His mom and dad wrote,
'Santa, we have a son,
Whose life's underwater.
Now that's not much fun!

'Our Jim's missed so much
and we want him to know
We'll celebrate Christmas
when he returns home!

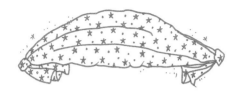

'All of his presents
wait under the tree;
There'll be turkey and lamb
for the whole family!'"

"You know what this means,"
St. Nick said with a grin,
"Boys, when was the last time
we went for a swim?

"We know young Jim serves
in a nuke submarine,
We'll appear on its sonar—
perhaps make a scene!"

Then, scuba gear on
and with a great splash,
They dived in the ocean
as quick as a flash!

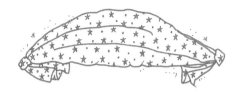

While tracking the sub's screen,
Jim heard a strong bleep,
Then spotted a strange sight
in the great briny deep!

He heard a faint tapping
on the sub wall outside,
"It's Morse code for me,"
Jim excitedly cried.

"Nick's sending a message
from family at home:
'We'll always be with you
wherever you roam.'"

Jim thought, "At this Christmas
we must be apart,
But we'll all be together
down deep in my heart.

"And there in my quarters
I have a small tree,
With gifts for each one of them,
chosen by me."

Now, after this visit
and on through the night,
St. Nick and his deer
saw incredible sights:

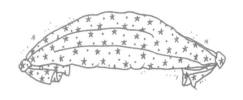

A bomber called Stealth
and a Black Hawk and Cobra,
Then, carriers and AWACS
(which made Nick quite sober).

He knew soldiers and sailors
who served proudly on these:
Spec Forces and Rangers,
Commandos and SEALs.

Nick met with them all
and was truly inspired,
Their courage, integrity,
he greatly admired.